JUV
F
TRY

ALBERT'S ALPHABET

by Leslie Tryon

Aladdin Paperbacks

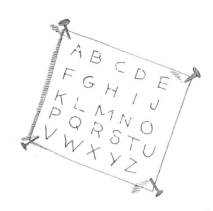

Special thanks to J, Eva, Con, Joy, Jo Ellen, Bev, and Gary

Aladdin Paperbacks
An imprint of Simon & Schuster
Children's Publishing Division
1230 Avenue of the Americas
New York, NY 10020
Copyright © 1991 by Leslie Tryon
All rights reserved including the right of reproduction
in whole or in part in any form.
First Aladdin Paperbacks edition, 1994
Also available in a hardcover edition from
Atheneum Books for Young Readers
Printed in the United States of America
10   9   8   7   6   5   4   3   2
Library of Congress Cataloging-in-Publication Data
Tryon, Leslie.
Albert's alphabet / by Leslie Tryon. – 1st Aladdin Books ed.
p.   cm.
Summary: Clever Albert uses all the supplies in his workshop to build an
alphabet for the school playground.
ISBN 0-689-71799-7
[1. Alphabet.   2. Building – Fiction.   3. Ducks – Fiction.]
I. Title.
PZ7.T7865A1   1994
[E] – dc20   93-48408

For my parents, Dorothy and Lester

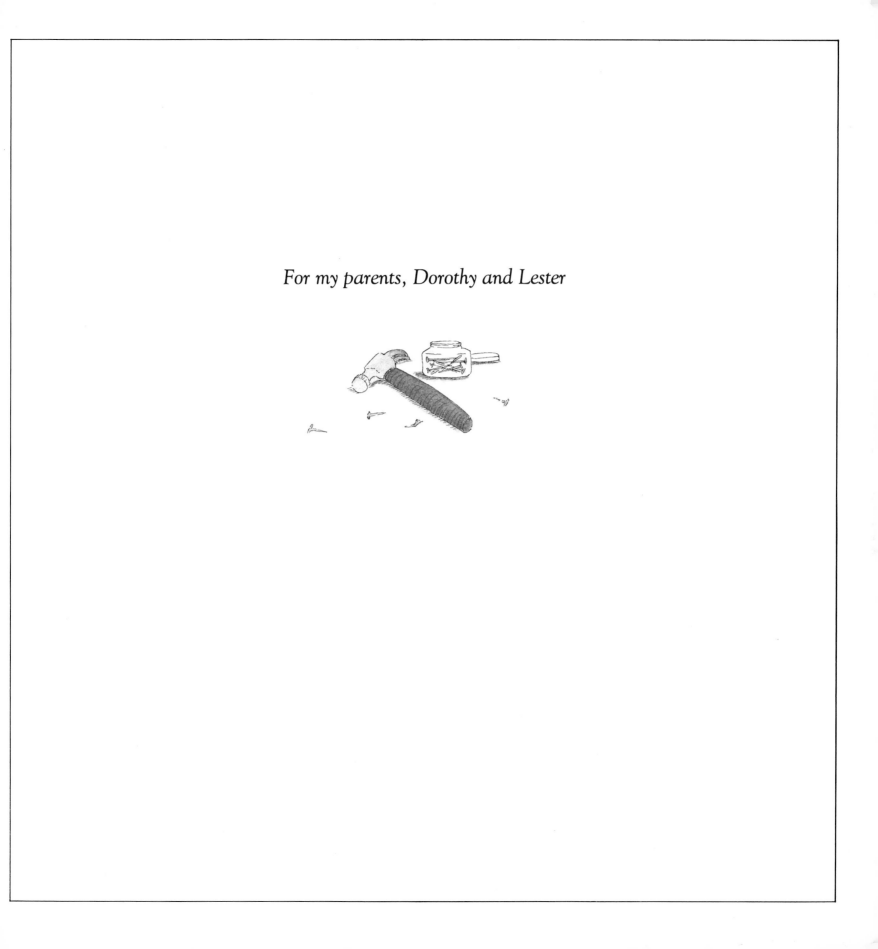

Note to parents and teachers:

Part of the fun of *Albert's Alphabet* lies in the fact that Albert so carefully plans and uses every scrap of material he has before moving on to his more unusual creations. Children often love to pore over such details, allowing adult and child an opportunity to enjoy the book together again and again. It is also fun to note that all of Albert's building techniques—with perhaps a *little* bit of license here and there—follow common methods for cutting and joining in carpentry. As for his solution for the letter "Z"—well, he had to do it somehow!

Memo to:
Albert
School Carpenter

Good morning Albert,

Please build an alphabet for
the walking path on the
school playground. We must
have it by three o'clock this
afternoon.

If you have time will
you try to fix that leaky
old drinking fountain please?

Thank you
Principal
Pleasant Valley
School

Does Albert have enough time?

Does Albert have enough materials?

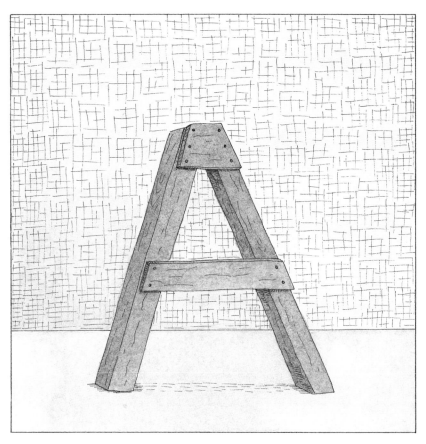

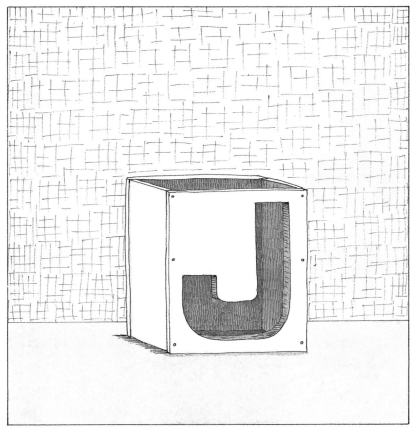

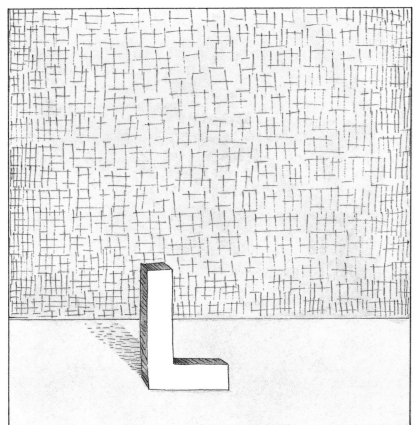

Oh Oh.
Albert used all of his lumber.
He used his box.

What will he use now?

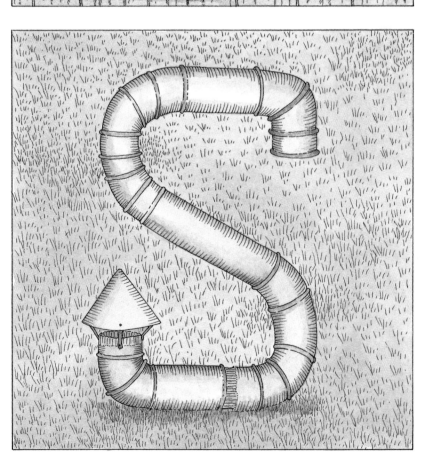

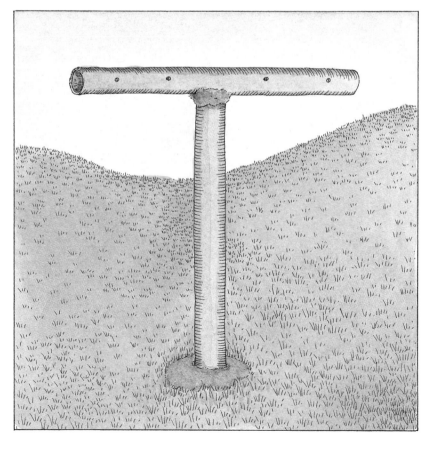

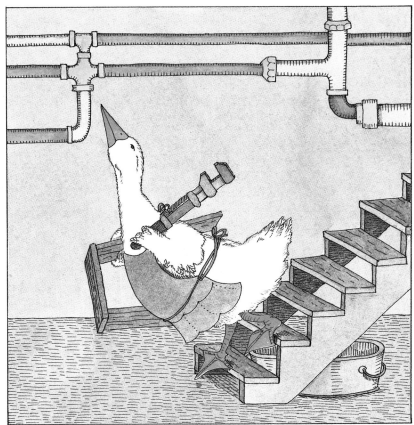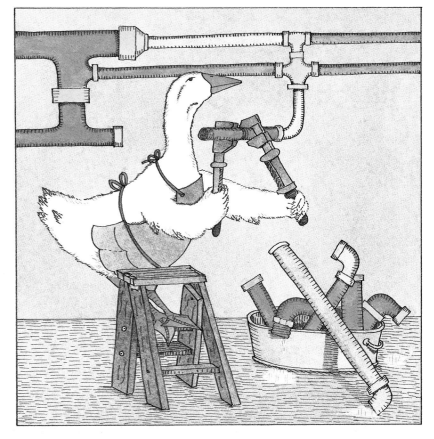

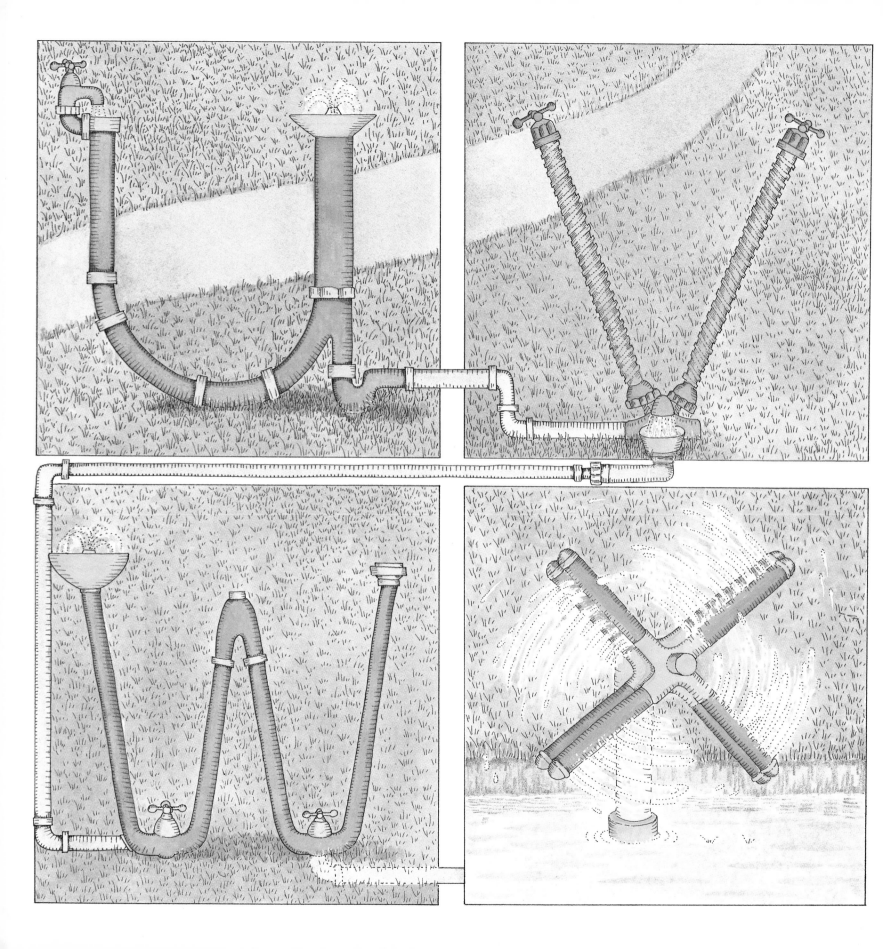